First Voyager Books edition 1996
Voyager Books is a registered trademark of Harcourt Brace & Company.

Library of Congress Cataloging-in-Publication Data
Nightingale, Sandy.
A giraffe on the moon/by Sandy Nightingale.
p.   cm.
Summary: The fantasy images of a young child's dream include a giraffe on
the moon, a cat in a balloon, and a dinosaur on skis.
ISBN 0-15-230950-0
ISBN 0-15-201348-2 (pbk.)
[1. Dreams — Fiction.   2. Stories in rhyme.]   I. Title.
PZ8.3.N5652Gi   1991
[E] — dc20   91-451

Printed in Great Britain
by Cambus Litho

This book was printed with soya-based inks on Leykam recycled paper,
which contains more than 20 percent postconsumer waste and has a total
recycled content of at least 50 percent.

A B C D E

A B C D E (pbk.)

A Giraffe on the Moon

Written and illustrated by

SANDY NIGHTINGALE

Voyager Books

Harcourt Brace & Company

San Diego   New York   London

I didn't expect
to see . . .

a giraffe
on the moon,

a cat in
a balloon,

a snowman on a
very hot day,

a scarecrow
soaking the
hayseeds away,

fishes swimming
in the sky,

clowns performing
in a pie,

WILDERMUTH

our school lunch
cooked by a witch,

an elephant in
a salad sandwich,

piggies on a
high trapeze,

dinosaurs traveling
fast on skis.

These things
are strange,
and yet it seems,
I can see anything
in my dreams.

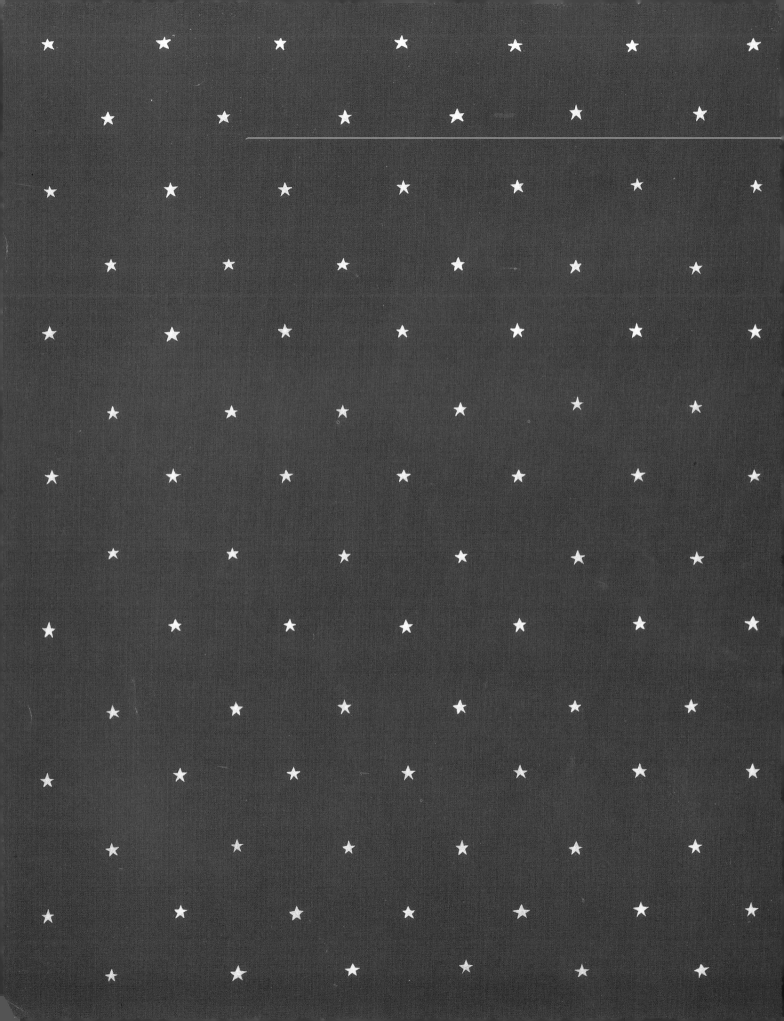